BOYS RULE!

Mouse Hunters

Felice Arena and Phil Kettle

RISING STARS

First Published in Great Britain by
RISING STARS UK LTD 2006
22 Grafton Street, London, W1S 4EX

For more information visit our website at:
www.risingstars-uk.com

British Library Cataloguing in Publication Data
A CIP record for this book is available from the British Library.

ISBN: 978-1-84680-055-9

First published in 2006 by
MACMILLAN EDUCATION AUSTRALIA PTY LTD
627 Chapel Street, South Yarra 3141

Visit our website at www.macmillan.com.au or
go directly to www.macmillanlibrary.com.au

Associated companies and representatives throughout the world.

Series created by Felice Arena and Phil Kettle
Project management by Limelight Press Pty Ltd
Cover and text design by Lore Foye
Illustrations by David Cox

Printed in China

UK Editorial by Westcote Computing Editorial Services

Contents

Josh   Con

CHAPTER 1

It's a Mouse!

Con and Josh are standing near the
tool shed at the back of Con's house.

Josh "What's your Dad swearing
about? He sounds really angry!"
Con "There's a mouse in his
tool shed. He's trying to catch it
before it eats the whole tool shed
and starts on the house!"

Con "I hate mice."

Josh "Me too, they're so creepy."

Con "Let's catch it."

Josh "What would it be like if the mouse ate its way right through your house?"

Con "Yes, I might wake up one morning to find the mouse has eaten my house and I'm sleeping on the ground."

Josh "I think that it would take more than one mouse to eat a whole house."

Con "Mice are really big eaters."

Josh "How do you know that?"

Con "Well, they must be, because they're always looking for more food."

Josh "Just like you!"

Con "Right, so how are we going
to catch this house-eating mouse
that's living in my Dad's tool shed?"

Josh "Well, we'll have to think like
great hunters do."

Con "You mean like hunters in
Africa who hunt lions and tigers?"

Josh "Yes, this'll be like being on an African safari."

Con "Well, we should get ready. Great hunters need to look like great hunters."

Josh "And great hunters need all the right hunting gear!"

CHAPTER 2

Getting Ready

The boys go back into the house
and pack their rucksacks with all
the things that they might need ...
Marmite sandwiches, drinks, cheese,
binoculars and of course, the world's
biggest rat trap.

Josh "Why do we need a rat trap?"

Con "Because that's what we're going to catch the mouse with."

Josh "But a rat trap is for catching rats."

Con "Yes, I know, but this mouse has to be as big as a rat … and anyway, mice are really just small rats."

Josh "So do you reckon that mice turn into rats when they grow up?"

Con "Of course. That makes sense doesn't it?"

Josh "No, not really. But anyway, what's the next thing that we have to do?"

Con "We've got to find out where the mouse hides in the shed."

Josh "Yes, we've got to hunt it down."

Con "We can follow its footprints.
That'll take us to where it's hiding."

Josh "You'd have to be a pretty
good hunter to follow a mouse's
footprints. It's not like an elephant,
leaving giant footprints everywhere."

Con "Maybe we could just follow its droppings."

Josh "If we do that, then we'll just be droppings trackers."

Con "There has to be a better way of finding the mouse."

Josh "What if we look through the holes in the wall of the tool shed and spy on it?"

Con "Yes, that's a great idea."

Josh "We'll be like 'Spy Kids' ... only we'll be mouse hunters."

Con "Then when we find out everything about the mouse, we'll know how to destroy it."

Josh "Cool! So how are we going to destroy it?"

Con "That's what we've got the rat trap for."

Josh "All we have to do is put some cheese on the trap."

Con "And as soon as the mouse steps on the trap ... *bang!*"

Josh "The trap comes down on its head and *squish* ... its brains go everywhere!"

CHAPTER 3

I Spy

Con and Josh find some holes to
spy through and start their mouse
stakeout.

Josh (whispering) "How long do you
think we're going to have to wait?"

Con (pointing) "Not long, look, there it is, sneaking along the wall!"

Josh "Wow, it's huge. It's just as big as a rat."

Con "Maybe it's already eaten half of the tool shed!"

Josh (whispering) "He looks like a really tough mouse. I think he'd be really good in a fight."

Con "But no match for great hunters like us."

Josh "I wonder who'd win a fight between a cat and this mouse?"

Con "I think that this mouse could beat any cat."

Josh "Yes, I think the only cat that could beat this mouse is a lion."

Con "And there aren't many lions around here."

Josh "After we catch this mouse we'll probably go to Africa and be big game hunters."

Con "That would be so cool! We could even have our own TV show."

Josh "We could call the show 'Big Game Hunters'."

Con "Yes, and the show would star us—Con and Josh—the greatest hunters in the world."

Josh "Well, perhaps we should start by catching this mouse first."

CHAPTER 4

The Trap

Con and Josh take the rat trap into
the tool shed.

Con "All we have to do is set the trap
and wait."

Josh "But, we've got to put the cheese on the trap first."

Con "You can do that."

Josh "How come I have to put the cheese on the trap?"

Con "Because if it goes off while you're putting it on the trap, then *your* finger will get smashed, not mine."

Josh "So how come I have to get *my* finger smashed? Why don't *you* put the cheese on the trap?"

Con "Because it was my idea to catch the mouse. You have to do *some* of the work."

Josh "I think that we should do this together. I can hold the spring back, and you put the cheese on the trap."

Con "Fine. Ready?"

Josh "Ready. Now, quick, put the cheese on ... done!"

Con "All we have to do now is wait."

Josh "Yes, soon that wild mouse will come along and *slam!* The trap will squash its brains out."

The boys take up position outside
the tool shed and wait patiently for
the mouse to appear.

Con "Look, look, look! There it is."

Josh "It's stopped! I think it knows
that it's a trap."

Con "Come on mouse. Take a bite.
The cheese is really tasty. I tried
some. I know it is."

Josh "Look, the mouse has changed its mind. It's going away."

Con "It must know that it's about to have its brains squashed."

Josh "Well, that was a great idea. How are we supposed to catch it now?"

Con "Look, it's back, and it's got two of its friends."

Josh "Its friends look a lot smaller."

Con "Maybe they're the baby mice and that's the father."

Josh "Oh no ... if we kill the father mouse then the baby mice won't have a Dad."

CHAPTER 5

What Now?

The boys sit up and look at each other. Now the thought of killing the mouse doesn't seem quite so appealing.

Con "Perhaps we shouldn't kill it. Maybe we should just tell it to go and live somewhere else."

Josh "We could be a different sort of hunter. We could just trap animals and then let them go, or maybe take them to a zoo."

Con "Yes, but I've never heard of a mouse zoo!"

Josh "Look, the big mouse is sniffing at the cheese."

Con "He doesn't know whether or not to take a bite."

Josh and Con look at each other and both start shouting.

Josh and Con "*Don't touch the cheese!!!*"

Con "Quick, we have to go and undo the trap."

Josh "So what are we going to tell
  your Dad?"
Con "We can just tell him that the
  mouse promised not to eat any
  more of his tool shed."
Josh "We can make a sign that says
  'Mice please stay out!', and hang it
  on the tool shed door."

Con "Good idea."

The boys race to the tool shed door
as fast as they can. Just as they get
there, they hear Con's father shouting.

Josh "I think your Dad might have gone into the tool shed."

Con "Yes, and I'm guessing he's just found the rat trap."

Con's father appears at the door of the tool shed. He's hopping and holding his foot—with the rat trap attached to it!

Josh "Well, at least we've saved the poor mouse."

Con "Now we can change the sign."

Josh "To what?"

Con "'Dad in tool shed—beware, bad language!!'"

Mouse Hunting Lingo

Josh *Con*

hunter A person that hunts wild animals.

mouse A small rodent that lives in the garden or infests houses and tool sheds.

rat A rat can be a person who eats your lunch when you're not looking or it can be a long-tailed rodent, resembling a mouse, but a lot bigger.

trap What hunters sometimes use to capture animals.

wild animal An animal that spends most of its time hiding from hunters.

BOYS RULE!
Mouse Hunting Must-dos

☞ Keep your fingers and toes well away from a set rat trap. Remember, if you get your finger caught in a rat trap it might break—then how hard would it be to pick your nose?

☞ Wear trainers when you're trying to sneak up on mice. They'll help you stay quiet.

☞ When you catch a mouse, put on gloves before you pick it up. Mice sometimes carry diseases, and if it's hungry, it might bite!

☞ Remember that mice are always hungry. Smart mice live in places where there is lots of food.

☞ If you don't want mice in your house make sure that you don't leave uncovered food around. Put a sign up at the front door that says "All food securely locked away".

☞ Block all the holes and places in your house and tool shed that mice might be able to get through.

☞ Try not to touch the cheese you put on the trap. Mice are really good at smelling and if they smell that someone has touched the cheese, they won't eat it.

☞ If you can't catch a mouse that has invaded your house, get a cat. Cats are the best mouse catchers in the world!

BOYS RULE!
Mouse Hunting Instant Info

 The biggest mouse ever seen was so big that it had a cat in its mouth. That mouse was at Disneyland—it was Mickey Mouse!

 There are more than 20 species of mice and rats.

 The house mouse is the most common pest in houses.

 Mice prefer to eat grains and seeds, but they will nibble on almost anything you leave out.

 Female mice can have seven or more litters each year, and each litter has five to seven pups (baby mice).

Mice make their nests in hidden, enclosed spaces. They often use newspaper, bits of insulation or other soft materials to make their nests. They even use string.

 Mice can gnaw through almost anything. They can also squeeze through cracks that are only 1 centimetre wide.

 Mice droppings are dark brown pellets, about 6 millimetres long. Mice leave them wherever they go.

BOYS RULE!
Think Tank

1   Do mice like cheese?

2   How many different types of mice and rats are there?

3   Why do mice have tails?

4   How can you tell where a mouse has been?

5   Who is the biggest mouse in the world?

6   What are baby mice called?

7   What's bigger, a mouse or a rat?

8   Are mice pests or pets?

Answers

8 They can be both.

7 A rat is bigger than a mouse.

6 Baby mice are called pups.

5 Mickey Mouse is the biggest mouse in the world.

4 Mice leave mice droppings wherever they've been.

3 Nobody knows, but they would look funny if they didn't.

2 There are more than 20 different types of mice and rats.

1 Yes, just like we love chocolate.

How did you score?

- If you got all 8 answers correct, then you're ready to be a full-time mouse hunter.

- If you got 6 answers correct, then you might need some help if you want to catch mice. They can be pretty tricky.

- If you got fewer than 4 answers correct, then you should never try to catch mice! Perhaps you should keep some as pets instead.

Felice → ← Phil

Hi Guys!

We have heaps of fun reading and want you to, too. We both believe that being a good reader is really important and so cool.

Try out our suggestions to help you have fun as you read.

At school, why don't you use "Mouse Hunters" as a play and you and your friends can be the actors. Bring some binoculars and plenty of food for your adventure. Has anyone got any toy mice? And, of course, don't forget to bring a rat trap!

So ... have you decided who is going to be Con and who is going to be Josh? Now, with your friends, read and act out our story in front of the class.

We have a lot of fun when we go to schools and read our stories. After we finish the children all clap really loudly. When you've finished your play your classmates will do the same. Just remember to look out the window—there might be a talent scout from a television channel watching you!

Reading at home is really important and a lot of fun as well.

Take our books home and get someone in your family to read them with you. Maybe they can take on a part in the story.

Remember, reading is fun.

So, as the frog in the local pond would say, Read-it!

And remember, Boys Rule!

When We Were Kids

BOYS RULE!

Felice

Phil

Felice "Did you ever catch a mouse when you were a kid?"

Phil "Yes, I set a trap next to my sister's bed. I thought I saw a mouse go into her room."

Felice "Did you catch the mouse?"

Phil "No, but I caught something else."

Felice "So, what did you catch?"

Phil "I caught her toe."

Felice "Then what happened?"

Phil "Well, I caught something else."

Felice "What was that?"

Phil "My sister's chores for a month!"

What a Laugh!

Q How do you save a drowning mouse?

A Use mouse-to-mouse resuscitation!

BOYS RULE!

Gone Fishing

The Tree House

Golf Legends

Camping Out

Bike Daredevils

Water Rats

Skateboard
Dudes

Tennis Ace

Basketball
Buddies

Secret Agent
Heroes

Wet World

Rock Star

Pirate Attack

Olympic
Champions

Race Car
Dreamers

Hit the Beach

Rotten
School Day

Halloween
Gotcha!

Battle of the
Games

On the Farm

BOYS RULE! books are available from most booksellers.
For mail order information please call Rising Stars
on 0870 40 20 40 8 or visit www.risingstars-uk.com

44